MY DOG
F.I.D.O.

Sue Cason

Illustrated by Clare Watson

SUPa
DOOPERS

sundance

A Haights Cross Communications Company

sundance
A Haights Cross Communications Company

Published by
Sundance Publishing
P.O. Box 1326
234 Taylor Street
Littleton, MA 01460
800-343-8204
www.sundancepub.com

Copyright © text Sue Cason
Copyright © illustrations Clare Watson
Project commissioned and managed by
Lorraine Bambrough-Kelly, The Writer's Style
Designed by Cath Lindsey/design rescue

First published 1999 by
Addison Wesley Longman Australia Pty Limited
95 Coventry Street
South Melbourne 3205 Australia
Exclusive United States Distribution: Sundance Publishing

ISBN 0-7608-6638-4

Contents

Chapter 1
My Uncle Alberto

"Phone for you, Tomas," calls my mom. "It's Uncle Alberto."

"I made something just for you, Tomas. Will you come and get it?" says Uncle Alberto.

"Yes, Uncle Alberto," I reply.

My Uncle Alberto is an inventor.
He invents all sorts of things.

A window washer.

A *very* mobile phone.

A clothesline that follows the sun.

As I run to Uncle Alberto's place, I wonder what he's made for me *this* time. I really like my uncle's inventions!

Once he made me a pair of jet skates.

Another time he made me an airplane bed.

And then he made me an automatic
breakfast-in-bed machine. Now that was
really great!

I open his gate and run up the sidewalk. I knock on the door. My uncle's robot butler opens the door.

"Hello, Tomas. Come inside! Follow me."

I follow the robot to Uncle Alberto's workshop.

"Hi, Tomas," says Uncle Alberto, giving me a big hug. "Look what I made for you."

There, in the middle of his workbench, is a funny little *robot* dog. He has big brown eyes, cute ears, and a pointy tail. He is beautiful!

"For me?" I gasp.

"For you," says Uncle Alberto. "His name is F.I.D.O.—**F**riendly **I**ntelligent **D**og **O**bject. Just give him a squirt of oil every day, and he will be your friend."

Chapter 2
F.I.D.O. the Robot Dog

"Well, Tomas," asks Uncle Alberto, "what do you think?"

"I love him," I answer. "Hello, F.I.D.O." I pat his metal back.

"Yip!" F.I.D.O. barks and wags his little pointy tail.

"Will he chase a ball and catch it?" I ask.

"He'll do that and more," says Uncle Alberto. "He'll do all the things a real, live dog would do—catch sticks, dig holes, even chase cats."

"Now take him home. I know you two will have lots of fun together."

"Thank you, Uncle Alberto," I say. I put my little robot dog on the floor. "Let's go, F.I.D.O."

We're almost home when F.I.D.O. sees
something exciting—a man on a bike!

It is a messenger riding past.

F.I.D.O. sees the wheels going around and around. Then his eyes go around and around. He runs after the messenger's bike, barking madly, "Yip, yip, yip, yip!"

The man gets frightened and pedals at top speed. But F.I.D.O. is faster. He bites the wheels. The bike falls over. The messenger falls off, and letters spill all over the road.

"Control your dog, young man," shouts the messenger angrily.

"I'm sorry," I say, grabbing F.I.D.O. and picking up a handful of letters. "My dog is new. I haven't trained him yet."

I hurry home, carrying F.I.D.O. all the way so that he won't get into any more trouble.

"What's this?" asks my mom.

"This is F.I.D.O.," I say. "**F**riendly **I**ntelligent **D**og **O**bject."

"Hmm," says Mom. "Alberto's really outdone himself this time."

She looks at the clock. "I need to go to the bakery, and I'd like you to baby-sit for your sister. She's just gone to sleep, so try not to wake her."

I check on my sister, Lucy. She's asleep in her crib.

F.I.D.O. sees her, too. "Yip, yip!" he barks. "Yip, yip, yip, yip!"

Lucy opens her eyes and sees F.I.D.O.

"Yip, yip!" barks F.I.D.O. He jumps out of my arms and runs to Lucy's crib. He jumps and barks and barks and jumps.

Lucy is frightened and begins to cry. "Wah! Wah! Wah!"

I try to catch F.I.D.O., but he's too quick for me.

In comes our mom. "What's happening?" she demands.

She picks up Lucy and hugs her. I pick up
F.I.D.O. "I'm sorry," I say. "I haven't had
time to train him yet."

"So I see," says Mom over Lucy's loud cries. "Perhaps you should take him to the park and start training him there."

Chapter 3
F.I.D.O. at the Park

So I take F.I.D.O. to the park near the zoo. "Sit, F.I.D.O.," I say.

He sits.

"Walk, F.I.D.O.," I command.

He walks.

I throw the ball. "Catch, F.I.D.O.," I say.

He catches the ball.

"Good dog, F.I.D.O.," I say. "I knew you could do it."

"Yip!" barks F.I.D.O. "Yip, yip!"

F.I.D.O. and I play catch all afternoon until I say, "This is the last throw, F.I.D.O. We'll go home after this, and I'll give you a nice drop of oil."

F.I.D.O. looks very pleased with himself. He wags his tail.

I throw the ball one more time. It goes behind some trees, and F.I.D.O. quickly runs after it.

I wait for him to come back.

I wait and wait.

And wait.

"F.I.D.O.!" I call. "Here, F.I.D.O."

But he doesn't come.

I hurry to the trees to look for F.I.D.O. I see him, but he's forgotten about catching the ball. He's digging in the garden. "Stop! Stop digging right now!" I cry.

He stops. But it's too late. He's dug lots of deep holes.

Along comes the park attendant. "Who owns this dog?" he asks.

"I do," I say. "He's very new. I'm still training him."

The park attendant is upset.

We kneel down and begin to fill in the holes in the garden. F.I.D.O. helps, too.

Suddenly we hear a scream. "Lion on the loose! Lion on the loose!"

People are running everywhere.

"Oh no," mutters the park attendant. "One of the lions from the zoo must have escaped."

Zookeepers with strong nets come running from the zoo.

They tell everyone to get out immediately because it is dangerous when a lion is loose.

People start rushing to get away.

The park attendant tells me to run. "Hurry home where it's safe. Take your little dog, too."

I pick up F.I.D.O., and we race through the park. We are almost at the entrance.

Zookeepers are looking everywhere in the park. They *must* find the lion!

But it's me who finds the lion.

Or maybe it's the lion that finds me!

Chapter 4
Yip! Yip! Yip!

"Grrrrrrrrr!"

The lion is standing in the entrance. He is *very* big. His eyes are yellow. He swishes his tail.

I look around for a zookeeper, but I don't see one anywhere.

"Grrrrrrrrr!"

My heart is thumping. I spot a tree, a tall tree. Can I run and climb it before the lion eats me?

"Grrrrrrrrr!"

The lion licks his lips.

My knees are knocking.

Suddenly F.I.D.O. jumps out of my arms. He runs at the lion, barking and barking, "Yip, yip, yip!"

The startled lion looks at my little robot dog.

"Roar?"

Then he turns and runs away, with F.I.D.O. nipping at his heels.

I think the lion is glad when the zookeepers take him back to the zoo.

"Hey," calls a zookeeper, "that's a good little dog you've got there. I bet he thought our lion was just a big, big cat."

I pat F.I.D.O. on his head. "Is that right, F.I.D.O.?"

F.I.D.O. wags his pointy tail. "Yip, yip!"

Sue Cason

Sue Cason lives in a small fishing village with her fisherman husband, Baz, and her children, Amy, Tim, and Tom.

Their dog, Henry, digs holes, steals shoes, barks at visitors, and smiles at burglars.

The family still loves him, but as you might have guessed, they haven't trained him yet!

About the Illustrator
Clare Watson

I'm very lucky to be an illustrator because I get to work with three of my favorite things: books, ideas, and children.

I like books because they give me new worlds to imagine. And they teach me about words.

I love ideas because they can be so surprising. Sometimes I draw pictures for other people's ideas. I hope my drawings help you to understand the words and ideas you are reading and to enjoy the book.

I often visit children at schools. I tell them how I come up with ideas and how I turn the ideas into pictures for books like this.